Harry and Hermoine Bedtime stories
                    A Snow Day

The large bed depressed unevenly, first on the
left, then on the right. There was an exchange
of low hisses, as blame was hastily assigned,
but then all went still.
"You wake her."
"No...you wake her...as it was your idea."
"Celesca...you're younger than me...Mummy won't
tell you off as much."
"Shut up, Soph. You know you're Mummy's
favourite..."
Hermione huffed to herself and stirred awake as
her daughters argued. "Girls, girls...stop
rowing...I don't have favourites. I don't like
either of you..."
"Mummy!" the girls chimed together, the first
time they'd agreed all morning.
"I love you both!" said Hermione, grabbing her
girls by their waists and pulling them to her
in a fit of giggles. "Now, where are my
kisses?"
She soon learned, as she was assaulted by them.
"That's better," Hermione grinned. "Now...why
are you waking me up on Christmas Eve? At this
hour?"
"Well," said little Celesca, bouncing on the
bed. "Daddy and Uncle Neville have gone to get
some carrots for Santa's Reindeer."
"Mummy?" asked Sophie, who was nine years old
and worldly in her ways. "Does Daddy know that
Santa isn't real?"
"Who told you that?" asked Hermione, sitting
up.
"I did," said Celesca, calmly. "Last Christmas,
see, when we had the Grotto in Godric's Hollow,
Santa had a lightening-shaped scar on his head,
just like Daddy. I knew it was him, just
pretending."
"Why was Daddy pretending to be Santa Claus,
Mummy?" asked Sophie.

"Well," said Hermione, mastering herself.
"Santa is very busy at Christmas. It's really
hard to get to every little boy and girl in the
world in one night to give them presents. So,
sometimes, when the workload gets too much,
Santa asks people to go into shops and things
for him. He gives the best presents to the kids
of those mummies and daddies that help him out
when he needs it."
"Oooh, ooh," said Celesca excitedly. "Does that
mean that we'll get the best presents, because
Daddy helped Santa?"
"I can't tell you that," said Hermione,
evasively. "You'll just have to wait till
tomorrow."
"But, Mummy," Sophie complained. "We can't
wait. We've decided."
"Well, you're just going to have to," said
Hermione, sternly. "It's only for one more
sleep...then you can open all those presents
under the tree."
"Can't we have just one?" Celesca begged. She
was so earnest, so cute, that Hermione almost
gave in to her youngest girl. But she managed
to stay motherly firm.
"No."
"Just a little one? Please?" Sophie pleaded.
"No, not even a little one," said Hermione
firmly.
"But, Mummy, that's really so unfair," Celesca
complained bitterly. "We opened the last doors
on our advent calendars today. Sophie had a new
Gobstones set, but all I had was a silly little
pill-o-pers stone. It's pretty, but it's
rubbish. It doesn't do anything. It's really so
rubbish."
"Yes, it is," Sophie agreed, lording it over
her sister. "Especially as when Daddy let us
open a present yesterday, I had a years' supply
of Chocolate Frogs."

"Oh, he did, did he?" asked Hermione, narrowing her eyes. "I shall have to speak to your father about that."
"Please, Mummy, don't take them away," Sophie begged. "I so love Chocolate Frogs. I had your card in the last pack Daddy gave me."
"Oh...really?" asked Hermione, blushing at her daughters' enthusiasm.
"Oh yes," said Sophie, keenly. "But Daddy traded with me for one of Nicolas Flamel. I hope you don't mind. I needed him. I've nearly finished the Alchemists Page in my sticker book. All I need to get now is Paracelsus...oh, and Daddy, himself, of course. His card is so hard to get, Mummy, did you know?"
Hermione grinned to herself. "Your father was always hard to get, sweetheart."
"Stop talking about stickers," said Celesca, crossly. "We are supposed to be going out in the snow."
Hermione sighed that the truth had outed at last.
"Okay, girls, let me get dressed."
"Yay!" Sophie and Celesca tweeted in joy.
"We'll get ourselves ready, Mummy, You'll see."
Hermione had serious doubts about that, but said nothing as her girls disappeared from the room. She eased herself from bed and looked out of the window. The garden was covered in a blanket of white. It was stunningly pretty and Hermione was stirred by a sense of festive cheer. She smiled to herself. Her girls would likely wear her out, but it promised to be a lovely day.
Maybe she could just perch some Christmas cakes on her bump and leave them to their revelry. That might work for her.
But things soon took a turn for the insane. A blonde-haired head popped around the door.
"Mummy...can we bring toys?"
"Just one or two, Cesc," Hermione replied.
"Okay." And little Celesca popped away.

"Look, Mummy," said Sophie, emerging in the gap
Celesca had left. "I've put my earmuffs on and
I'm wearing all my jumpers, as its cold
outside."
Sophie looked like she was dressed for a spell
on the moon.
"You won't need that many jumpers," said
Hermione, crossly. "You'll be too hot. Take
them off."
"But I cant pick which one I want," Sophie
complained.
"Pick your favourite," said Hermione, getting
irked.
"They're all my favourite," Sophie pointed out.
"Besides, it's not fair to the others if I pick
one out special."
"And look, Mummy," said Celesca, emerging from
her room. "I've got my dump truck and bucket
and spade. Should I bring my fishing rod, too?"
"No," said Hermione, her exasperation growing.
"They are summer toys. Not snow toys. Put them
back."
"But, Mummy..."
"Put them back!" Hermione snapped. "And get
dressed properly. Snow days are no place for
your tutu."
"But, Mummy, I like my tutu," Celesca frowned.
"I think I look pretty in it."
"You do look pretty," Hermione huffed, then she
turned to Sophie and frowned. For she was now
half naked and all her clothes were in a pile
at her feet. "What are you doing?"
"My jumpers, Mummy...they made me so hot, I had
to take them off."
"Can I just take my bucket and spade, Mummy?
I'd so like to build an ice palace for a
princess..."
Hermione slumped back and sat quietly against
the wall. For a moment, nothing moved but her
shoulders. Then, a minute or so later, two
pairs of little arms slipped around her neck.

"Don't cry, Mummy, we're sorry," said Sophie
softly. "Look. I've put my favourite jumper on.
It's the emerald green one, look, like Daddies'
eyes."
"And I'll just take my dolly," added Celesca.
"She likes the snow. Don't cry, Mummy."
There was a whoosh in the hallway and Hermione
felt herself scooped up into fierce, loving
arms. He was such a dick, he could always cheer
her up, even when she felt sure she should be
mad at him. He kissed her forehead and gently
smoothed her engorged belly.
"I've pulled a sickie for the next fortnight.
I'm sorry, Min, I should have given work the
finger months ago."
"Daddy!" Celesca and Sophie chorused.
"Right, I'm thinking Potter Winter Games," said
Harry energetically, kissing Hermione again and
turning to his girls. "Sledging, Snowball
Fights and an ice skating race around the pond.
Mummy...will you be the judge?"
Hermione smiled up at Harry, as Sophie and
Celesca whooped in excitement. Pregnancy made
her so hormonal, but he was so ridiculously
lovely he just made her melt.
"Are you really staying?" she asked gently.
"Hermione...I should never have left," Harry
replied. "If I ever make that mistake again, I
give you permission to hex me senseless."
Hermione grinned. "Okay. But I'll change the h
to an s. A girl has needs."
Harry swooned at her. "That works, too."

Hide and Seek
Harry and Hermione tip-toed into their bedroom,
stopping at the foot of their king-sized bed.
They were trying extra hard to be quiet, which
was certainly easier for Harry, as it was

Hermione's turn to carry the baby. The sleeping
infant huffed in his sleep, so much like his
mother, and Hermione adjusted the little silk
neck scarf she was wearing, so her son's death
grip in it was less likely to choke her.
Harry grinned at the picture before him. For on
his bed, poking out from the end of the slate-
grey quilt, which had obviously been pulled up
too far, were two pairs of little feet. One
pair had only managed to pull on one sock.
Harry grinned fondly at the scene. Little
Celesca was only six, and she'd not quite
mastered the art of dressing herself properly
yet. And her older sister, wiggling her
perfectly besocked toes next to her, in their
not-so-secret hiding place, was firm in her
belief that such lessons had to be learned
alone, as good training for later life.
Harry grinned at Hermione and they exchanged
nods, ready to be begin. Mimi, their black-and-
white kneazle kitten, circled their feet once,
like a furry chequered flag marking the start
of the game.
"Well, Mummy, I really don't know," Harry began
dramatically. "But I really think that this
time we might just have to accept it."
"But I don't want to," Hermione replied, with
equal drama. "I don't want to believe we've
lost our little girls! What will we tell the
Longbottoms?"
Muffled giggles crept from beneath the thick
quilt, quickly followed by a cross little shush
from Sophie, was was older, wiser and a much
better hider. Even if she did say so herself.
"But we've looked everywhere, Mummy," Harry
went on. "Our girls aren't in their beds -"
"Or in the shed -" Hermione added.
"Or behind the curtains -"
"Or under the sofa -"
"Or even in the oven," said Harry,
thoughtfully. "Which is a pity, because I was
quite looking forward to having Little Girl Toe

Pie for my dinner. I had the gravy ready and everything."

And ten little toes crept cautiously up towards the safety of the quilt hem.

"Well, Daddy, I suppose you must be right," said Hermione, sighing in defeat. "We've lost our little girls."

"Which is a shame," Harry added, ruefully. "I was just starting to like them, too. And they were ever so pretty."

"Don't worry, we can make you some more," said Hermione.

"But I don't think I can wait that long for them to grow," said Harry. "Maybe there's a shop on Diagon Alley that sells them."

"Yes, maybe," said Hermione, encouragingly. "Maybe we can buy better children. Ones who are really good at playing Hide-And-Seek. That's my favourite game. I don't think I can stand to have little children who are rubbish at hiding, you know. Not when I'm the best hider ever."

"And I was the youngest seeker in aÂ hundred years at Hogwarts," Harry added. "And the best ever, too."

There was a cross little huff from under the quilt.

"Did you hear that, Mummy?"

"Yes, Daddy I did. What do you think it was?"

"Shall I guess?" asked Harry.

There was a little giggle from the bed. "Yes, guess," said a little six-year-old voice, quickly followed by a nine-year-old clicking her tongue in frustration next to it.

"Okay. Was it a meatball?" asked Harry.

Another little giggle. "No."

"Was it a dump truck?"

"Nope."

"Was it a hippogriff, laying eggs in my bed?" asked Harry, in deathly seriousness.

"Hippogriffs don't lay eggs," said Sophie bossily. "They give birth to foals and then

keep them incubated for six months, in a nest
made from their own feathers."
Harry queried a look at Hermione, who nodded
back with an impressed grin. If Fantastic
Beasts and Where to Find Them was being quoted,
who was Harry Potter to argue with it?
"Well, I don't know what is hiding in our bed,
Mummy, but it's certainly a very clever thing,"
said Harry.
"You know, Daddy, things that can think for
themselves, and are that clever, can be pretty
dangerous," said Hermione. "I think you should
get your wand, just in case it jumps out and
tries to eat us."
"You're right, Mummy," said Harry seriously.
"Do you think we can handle this ourselves, or
should I call in some of the Aurors to take
care of it?"
"I was thinking of going all the way to Hit
Wizards."
"Hit Wizards...for a meatball?"
The quilt flew up, and a cross little blonde
head popped out from under it.
"Daddy...I am not a meatball!" Celesca
complained, her expression furiously, adorably,
cross.
"No, but you are found!" said Harry, jumping
onto the bed. "And that means being tickled for
a whole minute as punishment! And your sister
will be next!"
Celesca screamed into a fit of giggles as Harry
began his punishment. Little Sophie leapt up
and ran to Hermione.
"Protect me, Mummy. Daddy's going to tickle me
to death!" Sophie begged, looking with eyes
wide in horror at her sister, who she was sure
was being murdered by tickles on the bed.
"You're on my side, aren't you, Mummy?"
"I'm afraid not, sweetie," said Hermione sadly.
"You picked your sister over me, so..."
And with that Hermione, who had been hiding her
wand in her infant son's blankets, cast a

silent tickling charm, which sent Sophie sprawling and curling and rolling around on the floor, giggling so much that tears streamed from her eyes and she accidentally wet herself. Which turned the whole mood of the house to one of uproar, as Sophie began to cry in a very different way.

"Hey, come on, it's not so bad," said Harry, scooping up his eldest girl in one arm and wandlessly cleaning her soiled clothes with the other. "There. All better."

"Thank you, Daddy," said Sophie, snuggling into his shoulder and sending a dagger-laden look at Hermione under Harry's arm. "Mummy is so mean."

"Mummy just doesn't like to lose, sweetheart," said Harry, grinning over at Hermione, who frowned back and made a face at him.

"It's okay, Mummy, I still love you," said Celesca, crossing to Hermione and wrapping around her leg in a deep hug.

"Well, that's good," said Hermione. "Because I was thinking, as it's still raining too much to play outside, we might have a baking day. You know how nice it is to sit in the kitchen and watch the rain, while smelling the smell of baking cookies. I was thinking oatmeal and chocolate chip ones today. And I need a helper in my kitchen."

"And I'm the best helper!" Celesca cried, holding up her hand by way of volunteering.

"You are not," Sophie protested vehemently. "I'm the best helper. And even more so because oatmeal and chocolate chip cookies are my favourite, so I'll help even better than normal! Tell her I'm the best helper, Mummy."

"I have room in my kitchen for both my favourite helpers," said Hermione, placatingly. Both her daughters seemed suitably pacified, though Sophie continued to scowl and pout and Celesca poked her tongue out at her in response.

"And just what am I supposed to do, while all three of my favourite girls are doing all this fabulous baking?" asked Harry, mockly affronted.
"You can take your favourite boy...and change his nappy," said Hermione, offering Harry his infant son. "It's quite a smelly one, too."
Harry huffed and accepted the sleeping baby, and the pungent aroma that came with him. He huffed again...he definitely should have offered to bake...

Grandma’s Visit

Hermione Potter fluffed the pillows on the bed one last time, then checked the clock. The big hand was nearly facing twelve now, which meant Grandma Granger would be arriving soon. Celesca Potter was excited, too. Grandma always brought her presents and Celesca wondered what she would get this time. She was almost as excited by that as she was her advent calendar window, which her mummy hadn't let her open yet.
"There, Mummy," said Celesca conclusively. "The room is all ready for Nanny Cat. We have tinsel in the windows and pretty flowers on the table by the bed. All I have to do is get my little oven and it will be perfect."
"And why would you bring your oven in here?" asked Hermione, lightly. "I'm quite sure Grandma wont want to cook after such a long trip."
"Oh no, Mummy, I'll be doing the baking," said Celesca, proudly. "I will make ginger biscuits, then mince pies, then chocolate cake for afters. Nanny can watch to make sure it doesn't

burn, then we will eat it all in bed while I
read her a story."
"And what story will you read her?"
"Daddy And the Basilisk," said Celesca. "It's
my favourite from The Adventures of Harry
Potter."
Hermione smiled at her daughter. "I'm sure
Nanny Granger will enjoy that. It's her
favourite story, too."
"I know," Celesca replied. "I read it to her
last time and she clapped when I finished. I
played all the parts, and I even pretended you
were in it, Mummy."
"But I wasn't," said Hermione, gently. "I was
Petrified, remember?"
"I remember. But I got Mimi to be the Basilisk,
and I looked at her in the mirror, then fell
down...like this."
And Celesca did. She fell down into a heap on
the floor. Hermione crossed to her and helped
her up.
"Now don't go doing that," she said. "You'll
get creases in your pretty dress. You don't
want to look messy for your Grandma, do you?"
"No, Mummy," said Celesca, jumping up from the
floor.
"Now, come along," said Hermione. "You can help
me tidy up downstairs. You know how messy your
Daddy is."
Hermione took Celesca's hand and led her
downstairs. The living room was a picture of
festiveness. Sparkly decorations hung from
every inch of the ceiling, the windows had been
sprayed with pretend snow and twinkling lights,
and there was a large Christmas Tree in one
corner that Sophie Potter was busy adding
baubles to. But she was very cross.
"Mummy, will you please kick Mimi! She keeps
hitting my baubles off!"
Hermione looked down at her black and white
Kneazle, who was happily pawing at a low-level

icicle tree-decoration. Little Celesca giggled
as she watched.
"I will not kick her!" said Hermione, sternly.
"And it isn't a nice thing to ask, is it Miss
Potter?"
"But she's ruining everything!" Sophie moaned.
"I want Nanny Cat to say how pretty my tree is,
but Mimi just wants to play with it!"
The Kneazle stopped and sent a dirty look at
Sophie, paw poised...then knocked the icicle
clear across the room. Sophie cried out in
frustration, Celesca hooted with laughter, and
Hermione bent down to scoop up her mischievous
pet.
"She just wants to join in and help with
Christmas," said Hermione, scratching Mimi's
chin as she purred. "Is that too much to ask?"
"Yes," Sophie replied grumpily. "Put a spell on
her to go away."
The Kneazle meowed in protest.
"Give her to me, Mummy," said Celesca, holding
out her stubby little arms. "She can help me
open my advent calendar instead."
Hermione raised her eyebrows at her daughter,
then at her cat, who suddenly clung on harder
with her sharp claws. Mimi knew what was
coming.
"Okay, if you're sure," said Hermione, handing
the cat to her youngest girl. Celesca gripped
on tight, holding Mimi too strongly for her to
escape.
"Here we go," said Celesca, lifting her advent
calendar from the wall. "What did you get
today, Soph?"
Sophie flicked her dark-haired head from her
tree decorating. "I had fifteen liquorice
wands, as it's the Fifteenth of December."
"Ooh, I love liquorice wands!" said Celesca,
dreamily. "Can I have one?"
"No. I ate them all."

"Sophie Potter!" Hermione admonished. "You
greedy little Niffler. Fifteen wands?
Honestly!"
Celesca giggled at that, but Sophie simply
frowned.
"I am not a Niffler, Mummy. Niffler's only like
shiny things."
"Liquorice wands can be shiny," Celesca pointed
out, thoughtfully. "Because of all the sugar on
them, can't they, Mummy?"
"They certainly can," Hermione agreed. "Unless
greedy little witches eat them all and don't
share."
"I'll give you a wand if I get one, Mummy,"
said Celesca. "Because I'm your bestest
daughter."
"No you are not!" Sophie protested. "I'm the
one making the tree all nice and pretty for
Nanny Catrin. So that makes me the best!"
"Mummy...will you tell her I'm the best?"
Celesca cried.
Hermione sighed in defeat. "If you carry
on....neither of you will be the best and I'll
just have to get your Daddy to make a new
little girl with me!"
"No, Mummy! Don't do that!" Celesca yelped.
"No, don't," Sophie agreed. "Cesc and I will
take turns in being the best. How about that?"
"Deal," Celesca concurred.
"And why shouldn't I have another baby?" asked
Hermione, curiously.
"Because baby James cries all the time," Sophie
whined.
"And he smells of poop," Celesca added, causing
Sophie to erupt in giggles of agreement.
"All babies smell like that from time to time,"
Hermione returned evenly. "Both of you two
did."
"I never did!" Sophie complained. "You said I
always smelled of roses."
"You did," Hermione replied. "Once I'd washed
the smell of poop off you!"

Celesca rocked with giggles on the couch. Mimi
tried to make a dash for safety, but Celesca
held her firm.
"And Ally Longbottom says her little brother
smells of talc most of the time. Not poop,"
Sophie continued.
"Little Alison will learn the truth as soon as
Enola starts asking her for help with the
baby," Hermione explained. "Don't forget, Soph,
you didn't know Cesc was a poop-machine until
you insisted on changing her nappy."
"Urgh...oh yeah!" cried Sophie, remembering
suddenly. The memory of horror was evilly
delicious. "Cesc stunk, didn't she, Mummy?"
Sophie grinned teasingly at her sister.
"I did not stink!" Celesca retorted. "Not as
bad as you, I bet. Mummy, who smelled
worse...me or Soph?"
"Baby poo is baby poo, girls," said Hermione,
sagely. "It doesn't matter which baby's bum it
comes from."
Celesca giggled again, but Sophie looked
disgusted. "That's it, then...I'm never having
a baby. Ever. They are just too smelly."
"And noisy," Celesca nodded, just as baby James
began to wail from his cot nearby. Hermione got
up and went to change her baby, who was
typically ripe.
"Go on then, Cesc, open today's door," Sophie
urged, pointing at the advent calendar and
sitting down to watch.
"Okay. Mimi will help me, wont you, Baby Mim?"
The Kneazle looked dubious, but sniffed at the
little picture the with big '15' on just to be
compliant. Celesca used her free hand to flick
open the little cardboard door.
And chaos erupted in the living room.
First, there was a loud bang like a cannon
going off, then a huge cloud of smoke covered
little Celesca's blonde head entirely. Mimi
made a break for it, hissing angrily as she
scurried away to the safety of the kitchen.

Then, fifteen Chocolate Frog boxes flew out
from the advent calendar, surrounding Celesca
like a ring of little moons.
"Ah, Chocolate Frogs!" Sophie chimed. "They're
my favourite. Throw me one, Cesc."
"No. You didn't give me a liquorice wand,"
Celesca replied, stubbornly.
"But you were still in bed when I opened my
calendar," Sophie explained. "And I had to stop
Daddy eating all of them. You know how fat he's
getting."
Celesca giggled. "Yes, he is getting fat. But
I'm still not sharing."
"Please? Just one."
"No."
"If you give me a Frog, I'll let you put Merlin
on top of the tree," Sophie offered.
"Okay." Celesca gave a big grin and threw her
sister a Frog. "What card did you get?"
"Nicolas Flamel...again. Who did you get?"
"Ooh, I got Daddy!" Celesca sang. "Mummy! Look!
I got Daddy's Frog Card!"
"That's nice, sweetie."
"Did you ever have Daddy, Mummy?" asked
Celesca.
"Yes," Hermione replied thoughtfully. "I had
your Daddy years ago...and lots of times
since."
"You must really like Chocolate Frogs then,
Mummy," said Celesca. "To have had Daddy so
many times."
"I've had Daddy a few times, too," Sophie
added, nodding serenely.
Hermione scrunched her nose and huffed
silently. "That's creepy, honey."
"Why's that?" asked Sophie, confused.
"Everyone's had Daddy by now!"
Hermione simply shook her head and continued to
rock baby James, who was cooing on her
shoulder.

Just then there was a knock on the door. Both
Sophie and Celesca jumped up, just as Harry
entered carrying a big, heavy bag.
"Daddy! Nanny!" the girls chorused, then
clobbered both with hugs in turn.
"Oh, Min, stick the kettle on," said Harry,
moving over to kiss his wife on the cheek. "I'm
sure your Mum could murder a cup of tea just
now. I know I could."
Harry winked at Hermione, who just glared at
him good-naturedly.
"Yes, Hermione, you give me that gorgeous
little boy in your arms and Harry can take my
bags upstairs," said Catrin Granger, ruffling
Celesca's hair where she was gripped, limpet-
like, to her thigh. "And then we can all have
tea."
"Nanny, I'll make you tea," said Celesca. "I've
got it all ready for you in your room. Come on,
Daddy. I'll make you tea, too."
"Ah, a day off!" Hermione grinned. "I knew I
had children for a reason."
"I don't want tea," said Sophie, haughtily.
"But when you are done, Nanny, you can come and
see the prettiest Christmas Tree ever! It'll be
much nicer than any tea."
Celesca poked her tongue at her sister and led
Grandma Granger and Harry upstairs to Grandma's
room.
"Oh, this is perfect!" said Grandma, happily.
"With the tinsel and the flowers...it's just
right."
"I picked the flowers," said Celesca, proudly.
"And Mummy got a big vase and put some water in
it and then I put the flowers in."
"And very pretty they are, too," said Grandma.
"Now, where's this tea?"
Harry flicked his wand at the toy stove and
there was suddenly a tray with a tea pot and
two china cups. Celesca very carefully lifted
the tea pot and filled the two cups. She tried
not to be too tickled by her Daddy's silent

spell when it settled lightly on her. It made
sure she didn't burn herself by accident. Then
Celesca handed a cup to Grandma and one to
Daddy, and took a box of orange juice for
herself, because tea was horrible and only
grown-ups liked it. Then Daddy swished his wand
again and magicked a little bottle of milk, so
that Grandma could feed baby James.
Once they'd drunk their tea, and ate all the
ginger biscuits from Celesca's oven, they were
far too full for anything else, so Celesca
climbed up into Grandma's lap to read the
story. In it, her Daddy was very brave, saving
a very naughty girl from a giant serpent, and
when her Mummy woke up - after her Daddy kissed
her back to life - they all clapped and
cheered, for even Daddy preferred Celesca's
pretend version of the story. Even baby James
burped happily.
"And we all lived happily ever after," Celesca
said, finishing the story and smiling widely.
"Daddy - were you very scared of the big
snake?"
"Well," Harry began, thoughtfully. "It was a
very big snake. All slimy and wriggly. But I
knew your Mum would tell me off if I didn't
save her, so I thought I ought to, no matter
how scary it was."
"Yes, Mummy would have been cross if the snake
had eaten her, I think," Celesca nodded,
wisely. "I'm glad you saved her."
"So am I," Harry grinned. "Just so she could
have three wriggly children with me!"
"I am not wriggly!" Celesca complained.
"But this one is," said Grandma, rocking James
gently. "And there's a little girl downstairs
who will be very stompy if we don't do down and
see the tree she's been working so hard on."
Harry chuckled. "Yes, come on. Let's go and see
the tree."
"Ooh, ooh!" Celesca remembered, excitedly.
"Sophie said I can put Merlin on top of the

tree this year. Daddy, will you help me reach the top?"
"Hmmm, I don't know, you are very wriggly," said Harry, teasingly. "Tell you what, how about I make you float up there?"
"Oooh! Yes, please, Daddy! Will you? Please?"
"Alright, but you'll have to ask you Mum the wand movement...I think it's swish and flick...but I sometimes get it wrong...and I wouldn't want to drop you on your pretty head, now would I?"Â

A Present in Pictures

Harry and Hermione Potter left the Apparition platforms at the Ysgol y Dewiniaeth gates and made their way down the sloping path to the school. The all girls witches academy was already thronging with other parents collecting their children, and many of them waved cheerily as the Potters joined the crowd. Hermione was scanning the mass for Mrs Longbottom, who was her particular friend, as Harry scouted for their daughters instead.
It was just happy coincidence that they found them stood together.
Mrs Longbottom was holding her new baby and talking to the teacher, Miss Morris, while her daughter Alison played happily with Sophie Potter, the eldest of Harry and Hermione's children. Little Celesca Potter was swaying around on the spot and singing to herself whilst trying to work out which monsters the clouds most looked like.
That was until she spotted Harry.
"Daddy!" she cried, running to him and wrapping herself around his thigh.

Harry scooped up the little blonde haired girl and hugged her tight. "Hey munchkin. Have a good day?"
"Daddy, I am not a munchkin," Celesca complained.
"You weren't a meatball either, but I still think you look like one," Harry teased, tickling his youngest daughter.
Hermione moved to Mrs Longbottom and gave her a hug. "Hi, Ennie. How's little Neville Jnr?"
"Trying," Enola Longbottom replied. "He's lately decided that sleep is for other babies. I was just telling Miss Morris, here, that I'm on the verge of giving him a sleeping draught!"
Hermione laughed, but she wasn't sure if Enola was joking or not. She did look very tired. Hermione turned to Miss Morris.
"Bore da, Miss Morris. "Sut wyt ti?"
"Da iawn, diolch," Miss Morris replied. "Ble mae'ch babi?"
"Gyda fy Mam," Hermione replied. "Nid yw'n cysgu chwaith!"
Both women laughed at that. Miss Morris nodded impressed. "Your Welsh is getting very good now, Mrs Potter. And your accent is improving too. A bit too Cardiff, for my Valleys roots liking, but still much better!"
"Thank you," Hermione laughed. "Sophie and Cesc babble away in Welsh so much at home I thought I'd better try and learn. I'm pretty sure I haven't mastered all their back chat yet, but I'm getting there!"
"Well, I have prepared Sophie's End of Term report," said Miss Morris. "Top of all her classes I'm happy to say. I will miss her when she goes to Hogwarts, that's for certain. Such a bright and pleasant young witch to teach. So eager to learn."
"She gets that from you, Min," said Harry, joining the group. "Bore da, Miss Morris."
"Bore da, Mr Potter," Miss Morris smiled. "And I look forward to getting this one next year."

She grinned at Celesca, who tucked shyly into
Harry's shoulder. She was due to join the Upper
Primary School in the next year and was not
looking forward to it. Harry laughed at that.
"Well, Miss Morris, if you can manage to stun
her to silence so easily, I insist you share
the secret with me!" Harry joked. "This is the
quietest she's been in three years!"
Hermione laughed as she came up and stroked her
daughter's hair. "Come on then, let's get to
London then."
"London?" Harry queried. "Why are we going to
London?"
"You promised, Dad, don't you remember?" said
Sophie, coming up with Alison. "You said that
if I was top in all my classes at the end of
the year you'd take me to London to watch a
movie in the Odeon."
"Oh yes, I did, didn't I?" said Harry.
"You could have just done what that Betelgeuse
man did," Celesca pointed out. "And made Sophie
dance in the air. Not that she's a very good
dancer."
"I'm the best dancer!" Sophie complained.
"Better than you, anyway."
Celesca just poked her tongue at her sister
safe, as she was, in the arms of her father.
"No, Daddy, a promise is a promise," said
Hermione haughtily. "Besides, I've already made
us a reservation in Chinatown. I have a
hankering for Shredded Crispy Beef."
"Ooh, me too, Mummy!" Sophie cried, licking her
lips. "And I'm going to have spring rolls and
prawn crackers and noodles with beansprouts."
"You can have whatever you like, sweetie,"
Hermione beamed. "You've earned it."
"Ooh, can I have a cake that looks like a pig,
too? They're my favourite."
"Won't you want popcorn in the cinema too?"
asked Hermione. "You don't want to be too
full."

"I wont be, Mummy, but I want a little bit of everything," said Sophie.
"Can I have popcorn too, Daddy," asked Celesca, sweetly. "When Nanny and Bampi Granger took me to see Frozen they wouldn't let me. I had to have sugar free lemon drops and they were just not the same!"
Harry laughed. "I'll buy you some popcorn. Just don't tell anyone, it'll be our secret."
Celesca beamed widely, and made Harry pinky swear on his promise.
An hour later saw the Potter family emerge from the Ministry of Magic Muggle exit and onto the streets of London. Harry and Hermione hadn't used The Leaky Cauldron exit in years, as almost everyone wanted to talk to them if they went to the old pub. They didn't mind so much, but it was hard enough to get little Celesca to stay quiet at the best of times, it was near impossible when everyone wanted to babble along with her.
So they found themselves in that part of Muggle London called Whitehall, and had to hop a few stops on the London Underground to reach Leicester Square. Celesca was like her Dad, and loved the underground train network. Her favourite bit was tapping the little plastic card onto the sensor to open the gate which led to the platform. Her Daddy called it an Oyster Card, which confused little Celesca, as it didn't look like an oyster. Come to think of it, she didn't know what an oyster actually looked like. It might be a sort of Muggle monster, which got Celesca all sorts of excited.
Because she loved monsters and was dying to meet a real one.
Once they had a fun ride on the underground train, they headed back up the stairs and onto the street. Hermione gripped Sophie's hand very tightly, while Harry cast a clever Rein Charm on Celesca, which meant she couldn't go more

than three feet from him. This was because she
was going through a phase of madly running in
any direction she fancied, with not much mind
for where she might be going.
This was fine at home, but if Celesca raced
into a passing Red London Bus, then bounced off
like a rubber ball on account of Harry's
protective magic, it would give their secret
away to everyone. And neither Mr or Mrs Potter
wanted to have to explain that to the Men at
the Ministry. They were getting tired of paying
Magical Reversal Squad fines for such
accidents.
Hermione didn't like the Rein Charm at all.
"Harry, hold her hand, won't you? If she hits
the end of the Charm and falls over, it will
look suspicious."
"Relax, Min," Harry replied calmly. "Once Cesc
falls the first time, she'll come grizzling to
me. Then I'll kiss her scuffed knees better and
she'll walk quietly by my side without
prompting. Trust me, only reverse psychology
will work with our little Seer."
Hermione shook her head in doubt. Sophie turned
her haughty expression to her mother. "I wont
run off, Mummy. I'll stay right here and be
good."
"That's right, sweetie, you will," said
Hermione firmly. "Because there are too many
Muggles out here. I don't want to lose you. I'd
miss you."
"You wont lose me, Mummy," said Sophie
confidently, squeezing Hermione's hand. Then
her eyes lit up. "Ooh, look, there's a sale at
the Lego store. Can we..."
"No," Hermione cut her off brusquely. "But if
you're very good, I'll let you pick a new set
for your birthday."
"Ooh, will you!" Sophie chimed. "I'll be good,
Mummy, I promise. I'll be the best."
The Chinatown dinner was very nice, and at the
end of it all the Potters felt a little fatter

than before they'd went in. Sophie and Celesca
spent a good ten minutes discussing how fat
Harry was getting, while Hermione whispered to
him that all it meant was that there was simply
more of him to love. Then Hermione and Sophie
went to browse in the Lego store, while Harry
and Celesca got an early look at the films
being shown in the big cinema that night.
On the way, they passed a man doing magic in
the street and Celesca dragged Harry to watch.
There was a big crowd there, and most people
clapped at the tricks, but Celesca was not
impressed.
"Daddy, that isn't real magic, is it?" she
asked, a cute little frown on her face.
"What makes you say that?" asked Harry.
"I can hear in his mind," said Celesca matter-
of-factly. "He's hoping no-one can spot his
false sleeve, or the trick bottom to his box.
I'll go and tell him, I think."
"No you don't, Miss Potter," said Harry,
yanking her back as she made to stomp away.
"But Daddy...he's cheating!"
Harry eyed her curiously. "I saw you playing
Battleships with Sophie last night. You didn't
miss a single one."
"Yes...and?" Celesca asked innocently.
"Did you read your sister's mind?"
Celesca shifted guiltily. "No, Daddy."
"Truth?"
"Truth."
"Pinky swear?" Harry smirked.
"Will you cut off my pinky if I lie?" Celesca
queried.
"Yes," said Harry solemnly.
"That's not very nice, Daddy!" Celesca cried.
"Neither is using your special magic to win a
game against your sister!" Harry laughed. "Now
who was cheating?"
"But that was only a game," said Celesca
blithely. "He's pretending for real."

"It cant be real, if its just pretend," said
Harry, sagely. "But, how do you know he cant do
magic for real? Maybe he's just doing a little
bit, so he can make some money."
"But he's cheating," Celesca insisted. "I could
show you, if you like."
"But maybe he's doing that on purpose, too,"
Harry pointed out. "Don't forget, I'm a magical
policeman. If he was doing actual magic in
front of Muggles, I could arrest him and send
him to jail."
"So you think he's doing pretend magic, but
making it look like real magic, only it's
pretend?"
"Maybe," said Harry. "But he's not hurting
anyone and it's fun to watch."
"Yes it is," Celesca agreed, nodding
enthusiastically. "I suppose that's okay then.
Come on, Daddy. We need to pick a film."
By the time Harry and Celesca reached the foyer
of the giant Odeon in Leicester Square,
Hermione and Sophie were already there. Harry
frowned at Hermione, who had given in and
bought Sophie a Lego Superheroes set.
"What?" Hermione queried in a whisper as the
family unit reunited. "Miss Morris told me
Sophie scored a hundred-and-twelve percent on
one of her tests...that deserves a reward in my
book."
Harry grinned at that. "Okay, you win. But I'm
not dressing up as Spider-man again. Last time
I looked like a Father For Justice and thought
social services were going to come knocking on
the door!"
Hermione laughed at that and gave Harry a
swift, amorous peck on the cheek while Sophie's
head was turned. She absolutely did not approve
of her parents being so kissy-kissy in public.
It was bad enough at home, where they could be
found locked together more often than a pair of
magnets.
"So, which film will it be girls?" Harry asked.

"Oh, look at that!" Sophie exclaimed. "Look, Daddy! They've made a film about you! It must be from where that horrible Squib, Miss Rowling, stole your life story notes from Rita Skeeter. Do you remember that, Daddy?"
"Yes, I remember," Harry frowned, crossly.
"Oh, look, Daddy!" little Celesca giggled wildly. "They've had to change your name, see, for the film...Larry Trotter and the Sorcerers Stone!"
"Sorcerer's stone?" Hermione scoffed. "What...don't they think people know what a philosopher is?"
"Larry Trotter!" Sophie continued to giggle. Sophie and Celesca fell about in mad hysterics. They even tried out their names with the new surname...and decided it was too funny to dislike. Even Hermione grinned at it, as Harry silently fumed. Hermione stepped forward to read the flyer blurb about the film.
"Follow the magical adventures of Larry Trotter on his first year at Pigsboil School for Witches and Wizards. Join his friends, Bob Beasley and stuffy bookworm Jean Puckle," Stuffy bookworm? Honestly?, "as they battle the Dark forces of Lord VolAuVent. Fall in love as Larry meets his destined soulmate, Jenny Beasley -" no, sorry, kids. You are never seeing this movie."
Harry laughed out loud as Hermione scowled nastily, then tore up the flyer and stuffed it into the nearest bin.
"Good, Star Wars it is then!" Harry smirked. Hermione rolled her eyes, but conceded. They approached the electronic ticket booth, and allowed Celesca - who was a tactile sort of child - to place the order onto the touch-screen, under Sophie's watchful eye. Then they moved onto the snack section, where Celesca got very upset and burst into tears at the Pick n Mix area. It was hard to make a fulfilling selection of sweets when you were only six,

little, and could only reach the bottom shelf. Luckily, Harry cast a swift Obscuring Charm, floated Celesca to her choices, and watched as she giggled happily, doing loop-the-loops while reaching for some jelly crocodiles.
Then they entered the cinema and sat at the very back. Then Sophie turned to Harry as the trailers came on.
"Daddy...you know how Disney makes Star Wars and Frozen now?"
"I do," said Harry, mutinously.
"Well, does that mean that Elsa can fly the Millennium Falcon and Olaf can get a lightsaber, now?" she asked, curiously.
"Never say never, honey," Harry fumed. "Anything is possible in Star Wars: Episode 19: The Death of a Franchise."
"As long as there's no Jar Jar Binks in this one," Hermione moaned. "I will literally walk out, I swear to Merlin. I might prefer Larry Trotter to that rubbish!"
"Even with Jenny Beasley?" Harry teased.
"Shut up, Harry," Hermione grinned back. "No talking in the cinema."
"Yes, Mum," said Harry, before cuddling his daughters either side of him.Â Â

What's Daddy Brewing

One of Hermione Potter's favourite places in her nice house was her office. It was big, had lots of important things in it, and was handy to be able to work from when she didn't feel like travelling all the way down to London. She didn't like the big city very much, and it was always too full of busy people. She much preferred to work from home, where she could keep an eye on things, and she could always

play with her kneazle, Mimi, if she got tired of working.
It had become especially useful when she and Harry decided to bring babies into their little family unit. When Harry was a member of Magical Law Enforcement's Field department, he was often sent away on very dangerous jobs to arrest nasty wizards who had broken the law. It was no place for babies. But because Hermione and Harry wanted to become the best Mother and Father they could be, Hermione had Harry help her build an office at home, so that she could carry on doing her important work for the Ministry of Magic and look after their little babies at the same time.
Soon enough, Harry decided he had arrested enough bad wizards for the time being, so he started working in an office, too, and sending other people to do the arresting for him. But Harry missed his wife and babies far too much, so eventually decided to build an office at home too, so he could help out around the house and he and Hermione could raise their family in the best way they could think of...together.Â
But Hermione's home office was bigger and had a lovely view of the big garden and the valleys beyond. It was very pretty, and it became one of Hermione's favourite things, to sit with Harry and their babies in the bay window and just look at it, while Harry sang lullabies or tickled whichever one of their unlucky children he decided on grabbing at the time. Later on, Harry had put up a swing and a long slide and a trampoline so that their girls could play outside and Hermione could watch them through the window while she worked.
This particular weekend was a 'working' weekend for Hermione. She tried to explain this to little Celesca, who was on the verge of getting upset that Hermione didn't want to eat ice cream with her, or listen to a story she'd made up about dragons with liquorice wands for

teeth, or to spend the day hunting for the
creatures in the cupboard or the ghoul under
the bed.
But the idea of a 'working weekend' set
Celesca's imagination on fire. She decided that
every other weekend must have been broken, if
this one was the only one that was working. She
skipped off happily, eager to see how this
would play out, thinking that if the weekend
was working properly, maybe the monster, who
she was sure lived in the pond at the bottom of
the garden, would come out to play with her
finally.
She was very excited by this prospect.
Her older sister, Sophie, meanwhile, had
decided she was going to set a new record for
everything that day. Her first record was going
to be building the biggest tower of Lego in the
world. So she got out all her blocks and tipped
them onto the floor of Hermione's office, just
as her mother had begun to read some reports
she'd just been sent that day.
"Sophie, sweetheart, can't you do that in the
living room?" asked Hermione patiently. "Mummy
has to work today."
"Oh, I'll be very quiet, Mummy," Sophie
promised faithfully. "But when I make the
biggest tower of Lego ever, you'll have to
measure it and send it to the Men at Lego for
their record books. And you ought to take a
picture and send it to The Daily Prophet and
Junior Sorceress, too. I'm sure they will want
to know."
"I'm sure," Hermione agreed with a little
smile.
Then Hermione went back to her reports. But
they were hard to read, because the click click
of the Lego bricks snapping together kept
disturbing her. She took a breath to be
patient, and rocked little baby James, who was
in a bouncy rocking seat on the desk next to

her. He cooed and gurgled contentedly and that
made Hermione happy.
Then Celesca came in.
She saw Sophie building her tower, which was up
to her shoulder by now. "What are you making?"
she asked sweetly.
"The tallest Lego tower ever," Sophie replied
proudly.
"Can I help?"
"No!" Sophie snapped crossly.
"Can I watch?" asked Celesca.
"You can watch, but you have to sit all the way
over there," Sophie frowned, pointing to the
very far end of the room. "And don't touch
anything."
"What about these two bricks?" Celesca asked
innocently, picking two up from the pile. "Can
I play with them?"
"No!" Sophie snapped again, trying to snatch
the bricks from her sister's hand. "I need
them. Besides, these are my toys."
"Mummy, can I play with the Lego?" Celesca
implored to Hermione. "I only want these two
pieces see?"
She held them up to illustrate her case.
Hermione sighed deeply, and put her reports
down once again. "Sophie, can't your sister
just have two blocks?"
"No, I need them all," Sophie replied
stubbornly.
"But isn't it nice to share?"
"No. It isn't."
Hermione frowned at Sophie, then looked over at
Celesca, who was stretching on tip-toe next to
the Lego Tower.
"Look, see, I'm helping," Celesca beamed,
struggling to connect the Lego bricks in her
very stretched arms to the topmost piece of the
tower, wobbling a little on her dainty toes.
"No! Get away!" cried Sophie, who snatched at
the bricks again, but actually pushed Celesca
into the tower, which came crashing down to the

ground. Both girl and tower hit the wooden
floor. The tower shattered, and Celesca bumped
her knee and began to cry.
"Sophie! Say sorry," Hermione demanded, as she
got up to tend to Celesca's bruise.
"Sorry? Why? She did it. She's ruined
everything!"
"She was only trying to help," said Hermione.
"I don't want her help! It was my tower!"
"Can't you just play nicely together?" Hermione
begged. "I have a lot of important work to do
today."
"No, I don't want to play with her!" said
Sophie crossly.
"Well then, I think you'd better go and play in
the garden," said Hermione sternly. "If you
cant be nice in the house."
So Sophie stormed off. Hermione gave Celesca's
knee a little kiss, told off the floor for
being so nasty as to hurt her, and Celesca was
soon as right as rain. She trotted off like a
bundle of energy, thinking that playing in the
garden was a very good idea. Hermione was
pleased that everything was sorted out now and
pulled back her papers again, to read all about
a new help centre for witches who were having
babies for the first time.
Out in the garden, Sophie was using the swing.
She scowled as Celesca came over to her.
"Go away. I'm playing here."
"You're swinging," said Celesca fairly. "I'm
going to have a go on the slide."
"I'm on the swing now," said Sophie. "But when
I've swung the highest any witch has ever swung
ever, then I'm going to go on the slide, and
slide faster than any witch ever has. So you
cant play on it."
"But can I play on it till you are finished
swinging, then we can swap?" asked Celesca.
"No, because you might break the slide. You
always ruin everything," said Sophie,
waspishly.

"I do not."
"Yes, you do," said Sophie. "Now go away. I cant swing as high when you're watching, cos you spoil it. And I reckon I can swing over the moon."
"I don't spoil anything," Celesca protested. "I want to see you swing. I don't think you can swing over the moon. No-one can."
"I can," said Sophie arrogantly. "Watch this!" So she swung and swung and went higher and higher. But just as she was getting very, very high, Mimi the Kneazle darted out from under a bush, chasing a mouse that she'd found there. Without thinking, little Celesca raced off in pursuit and didn't look where she was running...and she ran right in front of the swing...
"Oof! Ouch! Owwwww!"
Celesca cried out as Sophie came speeding towards her and hit her right in the face with her feet. She couldn't stop. Hermione, hearing the high-pitched screeching, came rushing out of the house at once, to find Sophie cradling her sister's head, which was bleeding quite badly as Celesca cried and cried.
"I'm sorry, Mummy, I couldn't stop!" Sophie begged.
"What have you been doing!" Hermione demanded crossly.
"I didn't mean to!" Sophie plead, tears welling in her eyes, too. "She was chasing Mimi and just ran in my way."
"There, there," Hermione cooed, scooping up Celesca into her arms. She cleaned the blood with a little flick of her wand and took away the pain with a clever little spell too, that Sophie didn't even hear.
Celesca stopped crying at once. "My teeth are broken!" she moaned. "Will I have to go to Nanna and Bampi to get them fixed?"

Hermione chuckled. "No, sweetie, just don't
tell them I used magic on your teeth to fix
them. You know how cross they get about that."
A deft spell later and all the damage was gone.
Celesca's pretty smile was as good as new.
Hermione sat her daughters down next to each
other and looked at each one in turn. "Now,
who's going to tell me what happened?"
"It was an accident, Mummy," said Celesca
quickly. "I was trying to catch Mimi and I ran
in front of the swing. Don't tell Sophie off.
It wasn't her fault."
Hermione smiled. "So it was Mimi's fault, was
it? Okay. I will only feed her dog treats for
being so silly and causing so much uproar. How
about that?"
"Okay!" Sophie and Celesca chimed, grinning at
each other that they'd got out of trouble.
"Now," Hermione went on. "I think we need to
find you somewhere to play where you cant get
into more trouble, and so I can get some work
done. I will get told off if I don't do it, you
know."
"I don't want you to get told off, Mummy," said
Celesca mournfully, hugging Hermione tight.
"No, we're sorry, Mummy. We'll be good.
Promise."
"Hmmm, I don't think we can take the chance,"
said Hermione shrewdly. "Where's your father?
Have you seen him?"
"He's in his Dungeon, Mummy," said Sophie.
"He's with Uncle Neville, remember?"
"Ah, of course," Hermione grinned. "Come on
girls, it's time your Daddy did some Daddying
today."
The Potter sisters jumped up and followed their
mother back through the house, after she
checked in on sleepy baby James one more time.
They wound their way past the kitchen and the
pantry, the alchemy room and the library, the
living room and dining room, and the second

library where Hermione put all her books that couldn't fit in her first library.
Then they went down the long spooky staircase, that creaked and groaned, until they reached Harry's Dungeon.
It wasn't really a dungeon, it was more like a cellar. There were rows and rows of wine bottles, and cases of brandy and port and all the other weird drinks grown-ups liked, but that little girls weren't allowed, but tried to sneak a bit of anyway when the grown-ups weren't looking. It was also the place that Harry and Neville came to make beer on the last Saturday of every month, which just happened to be today.
"Oh, hello, love," said Harry, as the door to the Brew Dungeon opened. "Girls...everything okay?"
"Your daughters are getting into all sorts of bother without you," Hermione confessed in a solemn voice. "Getting kicked in the face and breaking Lego skyscrapers. And Mummy just cant juggle all the drama and work at the same time. So I think Daddy needs to step up."
"But Daddy is working..." Harry offered rather weakly.
"Here you go, Harry. The Plum Porter is ready..." said Neville, emerging from the gloom with two foaming tankards of dark beer. Then his face fell guiltily. "Oh...hello, Hermione...er...how's your day going?"
"Fine...now," Hermione frowned. "Work, work and more work. You know how it is. And as Mummy's sort of work will actually pay the bills, I'm leaving our little cherubs to their Daddy for the day. Have fun."
And with that, Hermione turned on her haughty heel and sashayed away from the room.
Harry looked down at his wide-eyed, expectant children. "Well...I'm sure we can find something for you to do.."

Then the door opened again. Hermione had
returned with baby James in his high chair. She
placed him gently next to Harry's work bench,
then kissed him on the head, winked wickedly at
Harry, and sauntered away again.
"Daddy, what are you doing today?" asked
Sophie.
"Well, we were going to make beer," said Harry.
"We can help!" cried Celesca enthusiastically.
"We can make beer. I think. Soph...what is
beer?"
"It's a drink with naughty things in it that
grown-ups like, because it makes them be very
loud and dance a lot," said Sophie sagely.
"Oh, that sounds fun. We should definitely help
you make it, Daddy. It would be for the best, I
think."
"Hmm. The problem is, the first rule of Home
Brewing states: 'Always drink a home brew while
making a home brew'. And little girls aren't
allowed home brewed beer. Or any beer,
actually."
"Hey, Harry," said Neville mischievously. "How
about non-alcoholic cider?"
"Nev...that's just apple juice..." said Harry,
then understanding hit. "Ah...that's perfect!"
Harry flicked his wand and conjured two glasses
of apple juice, with ice and straws and
cocktail umbrellas, then handed one each to
Sophie and Celesca.
"Right, girls, you can do some weighing, can't
you?" asked Harry.
"Yes, Daddy!" they chorused.
"I weigh the best flour for cakes," said Sophie
proudly.
"And I always count out the right amount of
sultanas," Celesca added. "I do love sultanas."
"Excellent," said Harry. "Right then, Uncle Nev
will put two big bags of grain on table. I want
you to grab a scale each, and measure out
exactly one-and-a-half kilos of each one. Got
it?"

The girls nodded and rushed off to get the sets
of weighing scales. They had a silent row over
who was going to use the new one or the old
one, deciding in the end by a game of rock,
paper, scissors, which Celesca used her Seer
skills to cheat at and win. Then they set to
work measuring out the grain. Sophie was
concentrating very hard, which meant she poked
her tongue out and closed her left eye, which
was her little thing when she was thinking a
lot.
Celesca spilt most of her grain at first, as
the scoop was too big for her. So she brushed
up the little pile of dust and husks and put
them onto the tray in fron of baby James, who
ate them happily while babbling away in baby
language and overseeing everything.
Soon all the grain had been collected and Harry
and Uncle Neville put it carefully into the big
cauldron in the corner of the dungeon. Sophie
had to hold Celesca nice and still, as the
water in the cauldron was very hot, and if it
splashed onto them it would burn. But soon
Harry had all the grain in the water, so he
mixed it around really well until he was happy.
Then they just had to wait. It smelled like
baking and bread and porridge, and for a while
they just sat there without talking and enjoyed
it. Celesca closed her eyes and sucked as much
of the yummy smell up her nose as she could
manage.
Then Harry had an idea.
"You know, girls, seeing how Mummy was very
cross with me, and she's been ever so busy with
work today, how about we make her some surprise
wine?" he suggested.
"Oh, yes, Daddy!" Sophie chirped. "Mummy does
liked wine ever so much. The red ones are her
favourite. They make her cheeks go all pink and
she talks funny, which I like because it makes
me laugh so much."

"Is it like making beer?" asked Celesca. "Do I
have to get the scoop again, because I just
washed it and you should have said if I needed
it again."
"No, honey, it isn't like making beer," said
Harry. "Though you will need to take off your
shoes and socks."
"Why's that, Daddy?" asked Sophie, kicking off
her little white flats.
"Well you see, to make wine, you need lots and
lots of grapes," Harry explained.
"Like the ones you grow on the vines in the big
back garden?" asked Celesca.
"Yes, those ones," Harry confirmed. "Once we
pick all the grapes we need, what we have to do
then is get the juice out of them. And the best
way to do that, is to stomp on them!"
"Stomp on them?" Celesca cried, sounding
delighted at the prospect. She tugged excitedly
at her little yellow socks.
"I'll be good at this, as I'm a very good
stomper," said Sophie confidently.
"Yes you are," Harry agreed with a chuckle.
"You both stomp enough to be professionals at
it!"
"Here you go then, little stompers," said
Neville, grinning. "Come over here."
He poured several big sacks of grapes into a
huge round tub, which had a little spout on the
end. Then he lifted Sophie inside, while Harry
did the same with Celesca. The girls hitched up
their skirts, then began stamping and stomping
on all the grapes they could reach. The dark
little fruits squelched deliciously under their
heels and between their toes, making them laugh
and giggle.
"Eww, that was a fat one!" Sophie laughed, as a
grape exploded with a satisfying pop beneath
her.
"Look, if you dance on them, them squash even
better!" Celesca giggled.

So they started dancing. The vat was big enough
to do do-si-dos, and spin with linked arms, and
Celesca was little enough to do a sort of
frenzied can-can. Soon enough, all the grapes
were completely squashed. So Harry opened a
valve on the spout and collected all the juice
in a big glass jar, sprinkled some yeast on top
of it, then set it aside to bubble away till it
was ready.
"Mummy will be ever so pleased we made her
wine," said Sophie happily, watching the yeast
fall to the bottom of the glass jar.
"When will it be ready, Daddy?" asked Celesca.
"It will be a few weeks I'm afraid," said
Harry. "In the meantime, how about we take your
Mummy a glass of wine from a batch I made
before?"
"Ooh yes, she'll like that," Celesca nodded. "I
don't think she really wants to be working
today."
Sophie agreed. "Daddy, I think you should go
and tell Mummy to stop working, then we can all
go and sit in the garden in the sun, with our
beer and wine and cider with no naughty bits in
for me and Cesc. Then I can push Cesc really
high on the swing, and you can watch to see if
she goes over the moon."
Harry laughed at that. "I think that's a
wonderful idea. Come on, let's go and tell your
mother all about our little plan. I'm sure
she'll be over the moon about it too."
And, as I'm sure you can guess, Mrs Potter
really was.

Forty Clues
It's been an eventful forty years for Harry
Potter, now his wife Hermione wants to help him
remember some of them for his birthday. Only

the rest of the world, including his daughters,
have to pretend NOT to remember his special
day! Submitted as part of the HMS Harmony
Discord Writing Fest for Harry's 40th birthday!
***

For the longest time, Harry refused to believe
it. After all, this day happened every year. It
was as predictable as a Quartz movement,
occurring every twelve months - on the dot - at
the very end of July. So it shouldn't have come
as a surprise to anybody that it was
approaching fast, as the Summer drew on. It
just didn't make any sense.
After all, they'd never forgotten Harry's
birthday before ...
But as unthinkable as it was, it appeared that
this was precisely what had happened.
It started on Monday morning. Harry was sat
reading The Daily Prophet and enjoying his
first strong coffee of the day. Hermione was
double-checking that their daughter's school
bags were properly packed. Sophie had Quidditch
practice that day, so she had to have her
special dragonhide gloves, while little Celesca
had been chosen to help model the school
uniform of Ethel Hallow's Witches Preparatory
Academy, where she was always one of the best-
turned out little witches. Celesca was so
excited, so Hermione had charmed some pretty
little bows for her to weave into her blonde
hair, when the time came for her catwalk dÃ©but
later.
Harry watched it all and marvelled at how
fortunate he was. He looked at his beautiful
wife, his adorable children - the third of whom
burped and babbled away in his high chair as if
on cue - even their black-and-white kneazle,
Mimi, who was pawing prissily at her little red
bowl of milk in the corner of the kitchen. All
in all, he had very much won at life in his
opinion.

That's when things started to take a turn for the concerning.
Sophie kicked things off, by turning to Harry as she finished her cereal, and addressed her father seriously.
"Now, Daddy, you know how important a day it is on Saturday," she began. "So, I have to ask you a question."
Harry folded his paper and grinned at his eldest girl. What was she going to ask? What sort of present did he want? Would he prefer a new tie or nice pair of cufflinks? What flavour cake should they bake for his party?
But she didn't ask any of those things.
Instead she said, "Can I stay at Alison Longbottom's house? She's asked her Mum and she said it was okay."
Harry frowned at her slightly. "But don't you think that would be a bit inappropriate, considering what day it is? Wouldn't you rather be here with your old Dad?"
"No ... should I be?" Sophie queried, puzzled. "What's it got to do with you?"
"Well, I would have thought that was obvious!"
"Really? How has me and Alison buying our first training bras got anything to do with you?"
Harry nearly spat out his mouthful of coffee. "Excuse me? You're doing what?"
"Oh, Daddy, don't be such an old prude," Sophie cooed sympathetically. "It had to happen someday. So Ally and I decided we would do it this Saturday. It's not like there's anything else going on, is there?"
Harry coughed and spluttered and looked at his daughter, who simply fluttered her eyelashes sweetly and innocently back at him. Harry looked to Hermione in a desperate plea for support.
"Er, Mummy, back me up on this will you?" Harry begged. "This sort of thing is far too soon, isn't it?"

"What ... boobs and bras?" Hermione replied
simply, which caused Celesca to erupt in little
giggles at the breakfast table. "Of course not.
Sophie is a growing girl. I had my first bra
when I was eleven, and our little cherub isn't
far off that herself now. I think it's a very
grown-up thing to do."
"Grown up! Grown up!" Harry protested lowly.
"She's ten! She's just a little girl!"
"And now she needs to start thinking about big
girl underwear," Hermione pointed out
patiently.
"But ... but ... bras? Really?"
"Dont worry, Daddy, I don't have any boobies
yet ... or do I? They might have come today,"
Celesca began soothingly, only to look down her
school blouse to check. "No, I don't. I'll be
your bestest daughter now, Daddy. Don't worry
about Sophie."
Hermione looked fondly between her youngest
girl and her husband, who seemed on the verge
of a full emotional collapse.
"I'll always be Daddy's best daughter, because
I was here first and I've been doing it
longer!" Sophie protested, scowling at her
younger sister.
"That just means you've been doing it wrong
longer!" Celesca returned smoothly. Then she
poked her tongue out at Sophie, as Hermione
offset a row with a stern look at both her
daughters.
Harry rubbed his chin and the back of his neck,
his worry about his forgotten birthday bluntly
replaced by this new concern. Blimey, where was
the time going? His oldest child was becoming a
proto-woman. Harry wanted to stop time for a
little bit, just to enjoy her being a child for
a few years longer. Maybe Luna knew of
something in the Department of Mysteries that
could help. He'd have to ask her.

But then Hermione jolted Harry back to the
moment, and his previous problem took centre
stage again.
"Yes, Soph, you may stay at the Longbottom's,"
Hermione announced. "Mrs Longbottom and I are
going to Sally-Anne's Salon for the day anyway.
I need to get my French manicure touched up."
Harry snapped his head to his wife. "You're
doing that on Saturday?"
"Yes."
"This Saturday?"
"Yes. Why? Have I forgotten something?"
"I think you might have!" Harry replied in
pointed amusement.
Hermione frowned and moved to the calendar on
the pinboard near the fridge. She ran her
forefinger down across the dates.
"No, I don't think I have, honey. Thursday is
Bin Day, Friday is End-of-Year Parent's Evening
for Sophie - make sure you aren't working late
for that, Harry - then Saturday ... nope,
nothing happening then."
"It's July the Thirty-First!" Harry cried
incredulously.
Hermione scrunched her nose as she thought.
Then she lit up and exclaimed, "Oh, of course!
How could I have forgotten!?"
"Yes ... how could you?" Harry guffawed,
relaxing back into his chair.
"I have to take A Brief History of Time back to
the library!" Hermione declared. "You know, it
wasn't as brief as the title suggests. Thanks
for reminding me, sweetheart."
Hermione crossed to Harry and kissed him on the
head as he stared at her in disbelief. Before
he had time to answer though, Hermione had
bundled Sophie and Celesca out of the door,
wrestled baby James into his carry-cot and left
Harry quite alone wondering what was going on.
Things didn't get much better over the next
week. There was no mention of Harry's birthday
on Tuesday, and on Wednesday - when Sophie went

out to buy a present - it was only a huge box
of Chocolate Frogs to give to her favourite
teacher at her Parent's Evening. On Thursday,
even people at work were talking about their
plans for Saturday ... and not one mentioned
his birthday as part of them. The England vs
Morocco Quidditch match was being played in
London, and half the Ministry seemed to be
going. Harry, though, couldn't get a ticket.
"Sorry, mate," Neville apologised as Harry went
to his office to try and nab a ticket for the
match. "I just gave away the last pair to the
Malfoys. I cant wait to go, it's going to be
some party with all of us there. Anyway, aren't
you babysitting on Saturday? Ennie and Hermione
are having a spa day, aren't they?"
"Oh yeah," Harry grumbled. "But my Sophie said
she's staying with your Ally on Saturday. That
means you cant go to the Quidditch."
"Ally and Soph will be fine," Neville beamed.
"My Gran will look after them. She's not
completely senile just yet!"
Harry frowned at him.
"What is it, mate? You look troubled."
"I am. Do you know what day the thirty-first
is?"
"Yeah ... it's Saturday."
"And that's it? Nothing else interesting about
that date?"
Neville scratched his balding head as he
thought. "Nothing springs to mind. But I never
was any good at dates ... that's why I was so
lucky to manage to snag Enola as a wife!"
"Very funny," Harry frowned.
"You look pale, Harry. Why don't you take a
half day? Go home and have a lie down. Truly,
you don't look well. You seem to be lacking
your usual forty-tude."
Harry pinged his eyes to his old friend. "What
did you say?"
"I just said you don't look well," Neville
replied blandly. "It's not like you. Go on

home. I'll go up to your office and tell everyone you've gone."
"Okay. Thanks, Nev. I appreciate that."
"I forty you might," Neville nodded expressionlessly. "Bye, Harry."
And then he swept away. Harry rubbed his aching temples and decided he needed to rest. He was hearing things again. That always meant he wasn't sleeping. He had been working a lot lately, on a special project with Hermione, and he was burning the candle at both ends. Perhaps a few days off was just the tonic.
Especially if even he'd forgotten when his birthday was ...
On Saturday, when the un-remember-ed day arrived, Harry woke to a very quiet house. He was immediately concerned, as Celesca was going through a phase of being suspicious about the milkman, who brought them a dozen eggs with their milk delivery every few days. She point-blank refused to believe this was an amicable arrangement, and was led to further dubiousness by events at her last birthday party.
For Hermione had hired an entertainer - Coco the Clown - and part of his act was juggling with eggs. The problem was he was a very clumsy clown, and a very poor juggler, and he dropped an egg, much to the horrified gasps of the assembled party of children. Disaster was averted, however, when the egg bounced. The other children clapped, but Celesca - who had a peculiar relationship with eggs that didn't behave as they were supposed to - was suspicious.
So now, whenever the milkman delivered eggs to the Potter Household, Celesca got up early and snuck downstairs to investigate. Harry was often woken by his daughter's little voice in the kitchen, repeating, "no ... no ... no ..." as she 'tested' every egg for its bounce-ability ... and she soon became little 'Celesca Island' at the middle of 'Yolk Lake'...

But today, there was no such smashing sound. In fact, there was no sound at all. Harry was stirred to excitement, wondering if his little family was hiding downstairs and about to give him a surprise birthday breakfast. Yes! That would be it! He'd got them! But he had to play along, like a good Dad. So he dressed quietly, hitched his disappointed face back on and made his way downstairs.

But there was no gaudy banner, no eruption of 'Surprise!' as he entered the kitchen, no pile of presents next to a pile of bacon and sausages (they hadn't had eggs for breakfast in months, obviously). In fact, the house was completely empty.

For the first time, Harry felt mildly concerned. He searched the house for his family, but they weren't in either of Hermione's libraries, nor the living room or the music room. The cellar was empty, the shed bare, even the vast gardens were populated only by pretty plants. There was no sign of either of Harry's pretty girls or his even prettier wife.

Where in the world could they be?

It was as Harry was walking back down the hall that he received his first clue. Little did he know it would be the first of many. He was ambling back towards the kitchen when he saw, right there pinned to the door of the cupboard under the stairs, a letter in heavy parchment ... a letter with his name on it, written in emerald green ink!

To Mr H. Potterâ€¨C/o his first bedroom (sort of)â€¨Potter Manorâ€¨Brecon Valleyâ€¨South Wales.

Grinning widely, Harry grabbed the letter and tore it open. The letter inside was made of a similarly heavy parchment, but the handwriting was the undoubted neat calligraphy of his playful wife. So Harry read in deep curiosity.

Dear Mr Potter.

I regret to inform you that your beautiful wife
and children have been kidnapped by Forty
Naughty Fairies, who are threatening to tickle
them to death if you cannot solve a very
complicated riddle they have posed for you. But
- as we know you conquer 'Riddles' for fun -
this should be easy for you.
To begin the quest to save your wife, she says
you must start at the 'First Date'. Good luck!"
The letter wasn't signed. Harry read it again,
trying not to grin too deeply. The First Date,
Harry thought. That could only mean one thing.
Harry bounded upstairs to the bedroom he shared
with his wife. In his wardrobe, he kept a
Memory Chest. He knew Hermione had one too, and
inside they stored important tokens of their
life and relationship together. It was Harry's
idea, and the first thing he put in his was a
calendar of the year they'd first started going
out. Finding the first date on that would be
easy.
"January the first," Harry thought aloud,
flicking to the appropriate page. "Obviously
the first date ... but also when we had our
first date!"
Harry traced the date hungrily with his eyes,
and remembered how trembly and nervous he'd
been that night. But it all worked out
perfectly in the end. As Harry looked at the
page, he noticed the swirly mist of a memory
embedded into the page. Curious, Harry drew his
wand and pulled the memory from the calendar.
It was Hermione, revolving as if in a music
box.
Then she spoke. "Harry you have to help us!
These fairies just love to tickle us! Here is
your next clue - if I wanted to make a very big
dog sleepy, I'd probably play him Mozart!"
And then the little Hermione vanished as the
memory faded. Harry frowned. What on Earth did
that mean?

"Big dog? Sleepy? Mozart?" Harry mused. "What
does that ... oh, hold on? A big dog? Could
that be ... Fluffy? But what does she mean
about Mozart? Oh ... of course! Very clever
wifey!"
Harry smiled again and reached into a storage
trunk on top of the wardrobe. He fished around
inside and found one of his first ever presents
- a flute whittled for him by Hagrid. He took
it out, and gave it a toot, toot.
And a hidden attic door opened in the ceiling.
"My Magic Flute indeed!" Harry chortled.
Then Harry clambered into the attic. The sight
he found made him gasp and grin at the same
time. A large Devil's Snare was taking up most
of the space - probably courtesy of Neville,
Harry thought - and wrapped in one of its
tendrils was a shining silver key. On a dresser
next to it was Hermione's Memory Chest. Harry
was filled with a very old memory himself,
which broadened his smile as he cast a delicate
bluebell flame from his wand.
The plant reared back from the heat and flame,
dropping the key, which Harry darted in to
catch.
"Still got it!" Harry chuckled to himself, then
he opened Hermione's Memory Box.
It was empty, except for a castle from a
Wizard's Chess set. A little flag had been
erected from its ramparts - half white, half
green, with a big red dragon right in the
middle of it. Harry smiled fondly at it,
guessed at what it meant, then span into an
Apparition to the ancient Norman Keep of
Cardiff Castle.
Why here? Why was this important? Simple... for
it was here seventeen years ago, in this
picturesque location, that Harry Potter had
asked Hermione Granger to marry him.
Harry almost expected Hermione to be waiting
for him, perhaps surrendering on one knee -
much as he'd done to her on that wonderful day

all those years ago. But all he found was a
pumpkin full of sweets. He took one - a sherbet
lemon - as he rested on the crumbling
battlements to think.
"Okay, so what does this mean?" he pondered,
popping the sweet into his mouth. "A pumpkin
full of sweets normally means Halloween ...
hmm, I wonder ..."
Harry trotted down the broken staircase, across
the old castle to the undercroft, all the while
listening to a memory in his head. One where a
soon-to-be dead teacher was screaming about a
troll ... before fainting.
And Harry raced off bravely to save the life of
his future wife for the first time.
Well, it was an undercroft rather than a
dungeon, but it did have a ladies toilet with
an out of order sign on it. Harry chuckled
deeply, then pushed the door open.
Inside the bathroom, Harry found a cauldron
with two vials of potion next to it. One was
black, the other purple. A note - again in
Hermione's familiar swirl - read "To go on, to
some 'reflection', pick a colour and stir in
seven times."
"Very crafty," Harry nodded as he read the
note. "Now - which potion did I take? No, wait
... it was the fires that were different
colours! That was almost a disaster. Now, which
one did I go through? It was the black fire ...
I think. No, of course it was."
Harry took the black potion and tipped it into
the cauldron. Then he grabbed the spoon and
began to stir. It was hard work, and with each
turn the walls of the bathroom began to move as
if Harry were turning a giant lever. After
seven turns, Harry was faced with seven
mirrors, each with a rough engraving over them.
"Ego, Lust, Gluttony, OBHWF, - urgh - Greed,
Avarice, Hearts True Desire," Harry read in
turn. "I think I'll choose mirror number
seven!"

So he did, pushing the mirror like a revolving
door and finding himself on the other side.
He was now in a gloomy chamber that didn't seem
to go anywhere. On the floor he found one of
Celesca's dolls ... but it had been altered.
Harry barked out a laugh as he saw that the
doll had been dressed in Gryffindor robes,
adorned with masses of hair and over-sized
front teeth. In one hand, a little mirror had
been fixed. In the other, was a small note.
"Pipes," Harry read, another memory flaring in
his mind. "Ah ... okay."
He looked along the walls and found three large
waste pipes, each covered by an access hatch.
There were clever etchings on them - here a
badger, there an eagle, and on the last one - a
serpent. Harry shook his head good-naturedly
again, before focusing on the serpent and
drawing his Parseltongue to the surface.
"Open!" he hissed. The hatch obeyed, and Harry
made his way along it.
He was in another dark chamber and as he
started to cross it he kicked something on the
floor. He had to laugh again. It was a little
diary with a hole in it. Harry opened to the
first page where, written by Celesca in one of
her crayons, were the words,
"Help will always be given to those Potters who
ask for it on their birthdays!"
Harry chortled deeply, then called out, "I am
Harry Potter, today is my birthday, and I am
asking for help to rescue my family from
tickling pixies!"
There was a flash of flame above him and
Hermione's Phoenix - who was called Solaria and
had been Harry's wedding present to her -
exploded into the air, swept down, and whisked
Harry away in another burst of flame. She
deposited him at a dark transport terminal.
There, gleaming purple, was the Knight Bus,
waiting for him.

"All aboard!" called Teddy Lupin, who was the
new conductor. "Hurry, Godfather, I have your
ticket right here!"
"And where are we going?" Harry grinned.
"Who can tell?" Teddy winked back.
With a bang they were gone. Ten minutes later
and the Knight Bus skidded to a halt outside
The Leaky Cauldron. Teddy bowed Harry from the
triple-decker and the Knight Bus sped off with
another minor explosion. Curious, Harry stepped
inside the pub and looked around. It was empty,
except for Daphne Greengrass, who ran the place
these days.
"Ah, Harry, there you are!" Daphne smiled as
Harry walked in. "Your room is all ready for
you. Now, you do remember which one, don't you?
It isn't safe with all those Dementors and
falsely-accused murderers running about
everywhere!"
Then it clicked in Harry's brain. The tasks for
the Philosopher's Stone ... the Chamber of
Secrets ... this came next in the chronology of
his life! So that's what Hermione was doing! He
felt a great rush of affection for his wife
just then. She was so clever ... it was
probably his favourite thing about her. Harry
wracked his memory again, straining to remember
his room number. Then it came to him.
"Thanks, Daphne, I remember," he grinned at the
landlady, before mounting the stairs, questing
for the room with the shiny brass number eleven
on it.
Once inside room eleven, Harry began the hunt
for his next clue. He was loving this game so
far. He wondered where Hermione had come up
with the idea and what the next clue would be.
He tried to remember what had happened in
sequence, when he'd first lived these events.
Then, as if to jolt his memory, he heard a
little me-ow from the bed. He looked over to
see Mimi curled up with some kitten treats.

Harry watched her fondly a moment, for she'd
been dressed in a fluffy ginger coat. Around
her neck was another note, along with a
temporary collar bearing the name of her
predecessor.
"Aww, poor Crookshanks," Harry grieved,
recalling how upset Hermione had been when her
old pet had sadly passed away. Harry crossed to
his wife's new familiar, and unclipped the note
from her collar. "- 'July is lovely weather for
an ice cream'-. It certainly is."
Harry licked his lips, and a second later re-
materialised outside Florean Fortescue's Ice-
Cream parlour. The shop was nice and busy, and
Harry was sorely tempted by the sight of a
banana split at a nearby table, but it was
another sight that caught his immediate
attention.
For there was old Florean himself, holding
Harry's battered old Firebolt.
"This is for you," Florean smiled, handing
Harry the racing broom.
"And where am I flying it to?" Harry queried.
"Ah, I believe it is flying you, Mr Potter,"
Florean quirked.
So Harry flung his leg over the broom and held
on tight, as it suddenly took off at speed,
quite under its own control. Several minutes of
flying later and Harry touched down on the
messy, litter-strewn pavement of Grimmauld
Place.
"Okay, so this is the Sirius connection," Harry
thought aloud, feeling the usual pang at the
loss of his Godfather.
He pushed that down and headed up the stairs,
to the building that was once the seat of the
House of Black, but was long since converted to
the British Headquarters of the Society for the
Promotion of Elfish Welfare. A dowdy little elf
in a bobble hat and pantaloons bowed Harry
through the front door, where he was greeted in
the hallway by a sweeping cloud of silver mist,

that was distinctly Hermione Potter-shaped. As
it twirled and danced towards Harry, it said
something to him.
"If only we had more time ... if only we had
more time ..."
Harry grinned back and blew his spectre-wife a
kiss, which made her dissipate away. He moved
along the hall to the ancient Grandfather
clock, which had kept all the time it had ever
seen. Harry clicked open the glass covering of
the dial and inside found a hippogriff claw and
feather, which had been turned into a quill. It
sat poised and quivering on a piece of
parchment, so Harry drew his wand and set it to
motion.
The hippogriff quill began to write something.
Harry leaned in to read.
"In this house, my wings will never wither."
"What does that ... oh! I get it!" Harry
exclaimed, before vaulting up the wide
staircase to the attic, where Buckbeak had once
lived.
But the attic seemed to be bare, aside from
some piles of parchment. Harry was confused, so
sat down near the door.
"We saved Buckbeak ... rode him together,"
Harry remembered fondly, his cheeks glowing
with lovely emotion. "Then what good thing
happened next? Oh! Oh yeah!"
Harry began thumbing energetically through the
piles of parchment. On the third pile, about
seven sheets down, Harry found what he was
looking for.
HOGSMEADE WEEKEND PERMISSION FORM
I, Hermione Jane Potter, do grant Harry Potter
my loving permission to visit the village on
designated weekends. Should he wish to invite a
bookish sort of girl to join him, she
definitely would NOT refuse! Xxx
Harry laughed out loud, pocketed the permission
slip, and Apparated to the middle of Hogsmeade.

"Okay, now I'm stuck," Harry said to himself.
"We never went on a date in school time -
more's the pity - so where to start? I must be
here for a reason. How did year four start? ...
hmm ... how did all years start? ... or should
have started ... maybe that's it!"
So Harry headed to the train station. His luck
was in, for sure enough, there on a bench, was
an ornamental chalice. Harry looked at it
fondly, for on the base Celesca had written -
in a wobbly felt-pen scrawl - Try-Wizzerd Cup.
Harry thought it insanely cute that his
daughter had gotten the spelling wrong. Harry
approached the cup, which immediately filled
with flames and spat out a single slip of
parchment.
Harry jumped up to catch it, reading his own
name on one side, just as the cup vocalised it
in a deep tone ... or, at least, as deep a tone
as Sophie could manage. Then Harry heard
Hermione's voice, as she said -
"Where's the best place for a few 'rounds' of
toast?"
Harry beamed, inwardly and outwardly, before
practically sprinting to the grounds of
Hogwarts and that well-worn path, which he and
his wife had practically made their own over
the years.
But where to look next? The Great Lake was,
well, great. The next clue could be anywhere.
Harry scratched his chin as he thought. Where
was special here? The big tree? No, that wasn't
so personal to them, the orbital lake path too
vague. Then it hit him ... there was only one
spot Hermione would choose near here, and Harry
was at it in a flash.
To the casual onlooker it was an innocuous
bush, no different to a dozen others dotted
about the shore. But as Harry approached it, he
was blessed with two very different memories.
The first had him as a thirteen year old,
crouching out of sight in an adventure through

time. It was here, on this very spot, that he
thought he'd seen his father stand, only to
realise it was himself ... and that he was able
to cast a Patronus powerful enough to scatter a
hundred Dementors.
It was also the secluded spot where, on a balmy
April night some five years later, he and
Hermione would share their first kiss.
It had to be the right spot and, sure enough -
hidden beneath the brambles of the bush - was a
little Easter egg, in golden foil wrapping.
Harry chuckled heartily as he unwrapped it and
took the two halves of the egg apart.
"This had better not be full of crumbs or
something," Harry spoke crossly. "Or you and I,
wifey, will have a serious falling out!"
But Hermione Potter was not a crass and
thoughtless wife. Inside the egg, Harry found a
tiny rune dictionary. Perplexed, he cast a
spell to re-size the book and opened the front
page.
"This is the best tool to learn a CERTAIN spell
... especially when threatened by a dragon!"
Harry laughed again and pointed his wand into
the air with no direction in mind. "Accio Next
Clue!"
Sure enough, something flew at him from beyond
the trees. It was a small blue robe, that
probably came from another of Celesca's dolls.
Harry thought they'd been very pliant to have
been sequestered for this game ... normally
they kicked your ankles if you even tried to
move them around from their usual homes in
Celesca's bedroom!
The little dress had the next note pinned to
it. "Yule never guess where to look next!"
"Hmm ... yule never guess where to look next?"
Harry mused. "What does that mean? And the
dress ... ah, I think I know! I'm getting good
at this! You should have worked harder, girls!"
Harry hurried up to the castle itself. It
should have been closed up, but the huge front

doors were open and waiting for him. Harry
moved inside, looking first at the main
staircase - and affording himself a sweet
moment to remember seeing Hermione looking so
pretty there, as she had done all those years
ago - before heading into the Great Hall
itself.
Waiting just inside the doors, in identical
party gowns, were Padma and Parvati Hirani.
Parvati stepped forward and smiled warmly at
Harry.
"Good afternoon, Harry," she beamed.
"Congratulations."
"Finally! Someone remembered!" Harry cried in
glee.
Then Padma stepped close to her sister. "Yes,
congratulations ... on setting up the first
Squib-only Quidditch team. Isn't it a-maze-ing
how Quidditch can bring people together? Bye,
Harry."
Then Padma and Parvati skipped past him and
away, ignoring all his calls for them to stop.
"This is getting weird," Harry grumbled. "What
now? Okay, lets think. I've found the egg, had
the Yule Ball, then it was ... the maze! A-
maze-ing. Clever girl. Off we go again then!"
Harry happily span around and headed out of the
castle and back towards the Quidditch pitch. As
he expected, it had been turned into a little
labyrinth. Luckily the walls of it were just
low enough for Harry to see over. Keen to play
his part, though, Harry used his wand to cast
the four-point spell, and a directional charm,
and - even though it took over an hour this way
- Harry eventually found his way to the middle
of the maze.
There was a little stone plinth there with a
Gryffindor Prefects badge on top. Harry picked
up the badge and looked at it, seeing that it
had been altered slightly. The large golden 'P'
was still there, but instead of the other
little letters spelling the word 'prefect' they

now spelled 'Potter'. Under that there was a
flashing phrase that urged Harry to, 'Press
Me'.
So he did ... and he couldn't stop the smile
that crept onto his face for the next clue.
For the badge had changed to something that
Harry had almost forgotten. Instead of reading
Potter, it now said - flashing in much the same
way as another badge once had -, "Do you
remember the first time when a Potter REALLY
stunk?"
Harry felt his heart thud pleasantly at the
memory. He pointed his wand at the badge, and
muttered 'Portus'. A moment later and he was
whirled away, re-materialising at a small
picnic spot in Abingdon, near Oxford. There was
a little picnic bench here, under some towering
beech trees, which afforded a lovely view down
a wide canal in both directions. It was a
pretty spot, but it wasn't the sort of place
anyone would think of as monumental or
important.
But to Harry Potter it was ... for it was here,
on this spot, a stone's throw from Hermione's
childhood home, that Harry changed their
firstborn's dirty nappy for the very first
time.
And it really did stink!
Harry laughed deeply at the memory, and the
laugh rumbled on as he found, underneath the
bench, an unopened nappy waiting for him.
Written in yet more felt pen on the cover were
the words -
"Are you ready to do that for another one?"
Hermione's words echoed in Harry's mind, as
fresh as the day she told him. A second later
and Harry was standing on the very spot, on the
verandah of their Summer Cabin in Rhossili Bay
on the Gower Peninsula. He remembered the
moment vividly - he had been flicking through a
copy of Witch Weekly, that had an article on
baby-changing techniques, when Hermione had

pressed his hand to her belly and asked the
family-famous question.
Harry Potter didn't cry very often ... but he
had that night.
He wasn't going to now, though. There must be
another clue around here somewhere. For half an
hour he hunted around, but there were so many
possible places to look, so many great memories
that had been made here. Harry tried to pick
out one, but where to start?
"Right, we've gone through most of the big,
nice events of my life," Harry thought. "So,
lets go through what's happened so far."
He started ticking them off on his fingers.
Without realising he'd been doing it, Harry
noticed that he was counting them. He started
again and when he reached his current spot he
had counted thirty clues so far. The sun was
beginning to drop on the horizon now, and on
the wide beach down below a few groups of
revellers had lit fires for barbecues. Harry
could smell the wafting aroma of slightly burnt
sausages, and his eyes fell hungrily on the
grill on his own verandah.
"Oh, yeah!" Harry cried out, leaping up. He
suddenly remembered his thirtieth birthday,
where Neville had told him Enola was pregnant,
not a month after Harry and Hermione had
announced they were expecting their first baby.
They had all come to the Gower to celebrate,
and Neville almost set the cabin on fire when
he forgot about his burning sausages.
Harry whooped as he opened the grill and found
another note inside.
"You are getting very warm now, Harry. Thirty
of the Naughty Fairies have run away. There are
only 'tent-to-go'."
Harry grinned as he thought he understood, and
quickly turned into his latest Apparition. This
time he arrived at a private spot in the Forest
of Dean, where Harry and Hermione regularly
brought their girls for long weekends away.

Right there, billowing in the breeze, was their
magically-modified tent, red and purple and
gold in colour.
Harry hurried inside, thinking maybe his party
would be in there. But, alas, it was empty. It
looked as if somewhere had been there recently,
though, as the large table in the middle was
laid out with cards, as if someone had been
playing poker. Harry moved close and observed
the hands on display, certain they must be the
next clue.
"A full house, three of a kind, a king, a queen
and three aces?" Harry puzzled as he tried to
work it out. And then it came to him. "Hermione
must be the queen, and me the king, with the
aces as our kids, which also explains the
three-of-a-kind. And Hermione always says that
since James we have a full set, or ... a full
house. Oh ... I see ... James!"
Harry's eyes twinkled and his face flushed with
warmth as another memory came to his mind ...
of the night when he and Hermione conceived
their son. It had happened right here. Harry
hurried over to the king-sized bed in the
Parent's Pod at the back of the tent. Harry
looked at the bed, wondering where the clue
was. Then he thought he got it.
For the pillow wasn't the normal one that
should have been there. It was a fluffy child's
pillow with a niffler-shaped badge sewn into
it. Harry grinned as he looked at it, for this
was Sophie's special Money Pillow, one she'd
had since she was very little. She called it
the Money Pillow because it was the only one
that turned her baby teeth into Galleons when
she put them under it.
Harry felt a bit guilty as he thought that. For
it was his fault that the only time his
daughter had failed to turn her fallen-out
teeth into money had been when she tried it at
Hermione's parent's house - and Harry and
Hermione had gotten a little tipsy and did

husband-and-wife things - and the tooth was
completely forgotten about.
Sophie wasn't too upset, though, as she found
two Galleons waiting under her Money Pillow
when she returned home the next day.
Harry wondered if he'd have the same sort of
luck, and lifted up the pillow. It really was
his lucky day, as there, on the back of an old
wedding invitation, Celesca had scribbled the
latest clue.
"In the place where Mummy and Daddy were altar-
ed, you can see the stars."
Harry ran his thumb fondly over his daughter's
barely legible scrawl a moment, before leaving
the tent, and Apparating away once more. And in
the place he arrived now, Harry's heart was
positively alive with energy.
For he was standing next to a vast construction
- concentric circles of huge silver-blue
standing stones, all complete with equally
massive lintels. And at the centre was a
monolith that was also a ceremonial altar. It
might have been what Stonehenge looked like at
the time of its inception. Aligned to the
stars, open to the magic of the world, sacred
to the Goddess Luna, this was the Temple of the
Moon.
And it was here that Harry Potter and Hermione
Granger had become husband and wife.
Harry felt his heart thudding around his chest
as he made his way down the aisle once again,
fervent with all the same passion he'd felt on
that amazing day. He could hear the voices, the
cheers, see his beautiful bride standing ready
for him. It might have happened yesterday in
his mind.
But it was empty now, except for a replica of
their wedding cake on the plinth. A slice had
been cut for him, so he took a bite.
"Pumpkin sponge ... my favourite," Harry
swooned as he enjoyed the flavour of the sweet
cake in his mouth.

Then he looked down. In a small box next to the cake was a set of golden cufflinks, so joined together to look like interlocked wedding rings. Harry reached for them, reasonably certain about what was going to happen ... for the same thing had happened not long after he and Hermione had swapped those fateful 'I do's' about fifteen years ago...
So Harry picked up the cufflinks ... which became a Portkey ... and took him right to ... His own front door again.
"SURPRISE!!!!! HAPPY BIRTHDAY!"
Fireworks went off, party poppers banged, people cheered and whooped and yelled all sorts of Happy Birthday wishes Harry's way. Half the wizarding world seemed to be in his own gardens tonight, which had been decorated with lights and banners, balloons and real fairies. The Longbottoms were there, and Teddy Lupin, and Padma and Parvati waved enthusiastically at him. But Harry only had eyes for a small group of people who were hurrying up to greet him.
"Happy birthday, Daddy!" Celesca squeaked, clutching hard to Harry's thigh as he met them.
"Happy birthday!" cried Sophie, leaning on tiptoe to kiss Harry's cheek, before adding with a laugh, "I wasn't really buying bras, Daddy, I hope you know that!"
Then, finally, Hermione came up and kissed Harry tenderly on the lips, which drew yet more cheers from the crowd. "Happy birthday, honey. How did you like the chase?"
"Chasing you was always worth it!!" Harry grinned back. "I'll get you back for that on your birthday, you know!"
"Oh, you really wont!" Hermione laughed confidently. "Come on, the world and his dog is waiting to wish you a happy birthday. Besides, it's not every day you turn forty. Everyone's waiting to see my old man."
"Oi ... less of the old!"

Hermione laughed, their children laughed, and
Harry finally got his own party started.